Stuff We All Get

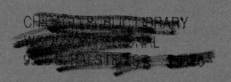
Stuff We All Get

K.L. Denman

Orca currents

ORCA BOOK PUBLISHERS

Library and Archives Canada Cataloguing in Publication

Denman, K. L., 1957-
Stuff we all get / K.L. Denman.
(Orca currents)

Issued also in electronic format.
ISBN 978-1-55469-821-9 (bound).--ISBN 978-1-55469-820-2 (pbk.)

I. Title. II. Series: Orca currents
PS8607.E64S78 2011   JC813'.6   C2011-903346-1

First published in the United States, 2011
Library of Congress Control Number: 2011929249

Summary: Fifteen-year-old Zack, a sound-color synesthete,
is on a mission to find a musician he relates to.

*Orca Book Publishers is dedicated to preserving the environment and has
printed this book on paper certified by the Forest Stewardship Council®.*

Orca Book Publishers gratefully acknowledges the support for its
publishing programs provided by the following agencies: the Government
of Canada through the Canada Book Fund and the Canada Council for the Arts,
and the Province of British Columbia through the BC Arts Council
and the Book Publishing Tax Credit.

Cover photography by Getty Images
Author photo by Jasmine Kovac

ORCA BOOK PUBLISHERS
PO Box 5626, Stn. B
Victoria, BC Canada
V8R 6S4

ORCA BOOK PUBLISHERS
PO Box 468
Custer, WA USA
98240-0468

www.orcabook.com
Printed and bound in Canada.

14 13 12 11 • 4 3 2 1

For Gary,
our geocaching guide

Chapter One

The office is a windowless gray cell. The vice-principal across the desk from me says, "A one-week suspension is automatic." He jabs a skinny finger into the air. "And if this offense is ever repeated, you'll be expelled from this school. Permanently."

He levels the finger at me, and his nostrils flare. "Do you understand, Zack?"

I nod.

"You'd better. Your conduct has placed you in a terrible position." He tells me to think about that. It doesn't matter what provoked me, he says. I shouldn't have acted as I did. Then he tells me to wait outside his office until he speaks to my mother.

When Mom shows up, she's still in uniform. The stink eye she gives me lets me know I'll be hearing plenty from her too.

As I sit on the hard chair outside the vice-principal's door, I can't help but think about my "terrible position." It sucks.

I've been in this town for less than a month. My cop Mom said we'd like it better than the last place.

"It'll be different this time," she said. I've heard that before. "I know you can make it work for you."

I've been trying to make it work. I wanted to play on the basketball team, but it was too late in the season for new players. I joined the lunch league instead. Yesterday I also joined them in wearing thong underwear. All the guys were wearing them, like NBA players, and when I tried them, I got it. They're perfect for basketball.

Play during yesterday's game was intense. People were watching and yelling from the stands. We were in the final seconds and ahead by only one point. The other team was on the offensive, and I was playing D. When one of them went up for a shot, I blocked him. I stopped the shot all right. But when he came back down, he took my shorts down with him. I don't know if it was on purpose or what, but my bare butt was out there.

When I reached for my shorts to yank them back up, I stumbled. I ended up hopping around trying to regain my balance. Everyone laughed, and someone snapped a picture. And the other team scored, so we lost the game.

The jerk who took the picture, Pete, probably had it online before we left the change room. By this morning, everyone at school had seen it. I didn't think many people knew my name, but they do now. And they've had a lot to say about my anatomy.

Even Charo, a girl who's been friendly, was giggling about what great pictures I take. One of the girls in her group asked if I wanted the photo to be in the school yearbook. Someone else asked if I'd pose for the flip-side photo. I got comments about cracks and cheeks. More than a few times, people called out, "Hey, Buns!"

It was all immature and annoying, and at first I tried to laugh along. I think the best I did was bare my teeth and go, "Heh, heh."

As the day wore on, it started to get old. I was gritting my teeth and grunting. It was around then that Pete found me in the hall. He was smirking as he walked up to me and said, "You owe me, Buns."

I looked at him and said, "Huh?"

He curled his lip. "You're a somebody now, aren't you? Thanks to *moi*. You either owe me for the picture, or you can give me something to make it go away. Your choice."

I chose to give him something. Bare knuckles to the sneer.

Punching him felt pretty good, but the teacher who was in the hall at the time wasn't impressed.

When we get home from our meeting with the vice-principal, I head into my room. Mom follows me, saying, "I can't believe you lost control like that. You're grounded for the next week. And I've got plenty of chores lined up to keep you busy."

Update on my position: the butt of butt jokes, friendless and now stuck at home too.

Chapter Two

Painting the kitchen walls isn't so bad, at first. I almost enjoy cutting in the edges with a brush. But when it comes to the rolling part, the work gets boring. Up and down, up and down. Flecks of orange paint fly off the roller and speckle my face, arms and hair. Yawning while rolling paint is a bad idea too. The paint tastes terrible. After a while, my arm gets tired and the orange starts to look ugly. There's way too much of it.

I'd like to put on some music, but that could be a problem. I have sound-color synesthesia, which is a fancy way of saying that I see colors when I hear music. Some synesthetes see colors for all sounds. They might hear a siren and see red, or hear a dog bark and see brown. Other synesthetes with their senses cross-wired see color-coded numbers. Some taste words, which I think would be bad. Imagine meeting a hot girl, then hearing her name and tasting dirt.

I see colors in brilliant flashes or in transparent clouds streaming through the air. They don't block out everything else, but they could interfere with getting the paint even. I do *not* want to get stuck redoing this job.

When Mom shows up after her shift, she's startled. She doesn't need to be a synesthete to feel the color. If the color orange had a sound, our kitchen walls would be vibrating with noise.

"Phew," she says. "It didn't look *that* orange on the sample."

"That was a dinky little square," I tell her. "Not a whole room."

"Good point," she sighs. "I think we have to do at least one wall over. In white."

"We?" I ask.

She shrugs. "I'll buy the paint."

"Thanks a lot," I mutter.

"Would you rather dig up the garden?" she asks.

"Oh, yeah."

"All right," she says. "It's a deal. Tomorrow you work on the garden, and I'll paint."

I think this is a good deal for me, until the next morning. I figured I would pull a few weeds out of the little plot in the backyard, but no. That's not it.

Mom stands in the yard rubbing her hands together. "Anything grows in this climate. It's going to be great. Lettuce, peas, onions. Tomatoes and potatoes."

"In February?" I ask.

"No, but we need to prepare the soil now. What else can we grow?" She answers her own question. "Carrots. Maybe some corn too?"

I stare at the puny garden and shake my head. "There's no way you can fit all that in here."

She waves her arm. "Not all in this little spot. We need to expand. See the markers I've put in?" She points across the lawn to where she's marked the corners of the new plot with rocks. "There are stakes in the garage you can use. Tie string between the stakes and that's the area you need to dig."

She's marked out half the backyard. "You're kidding, right?" I say.

"Do I look like I'm kidding?" she asks, eyebrows raised.

She doesn't look like she's kidding. "Maybe I'll do over the paint after all," I say.

"Maybe not. We had a deal, remember?"

"Some deal," I mutter. "Not like you told me what was involved."

"Not like you asked," she says. "Details are important. Haven't I always told you to get *all* the facts before you make a decision?"

"I never get to *make* any decisions. Why should I bother?"

She folds her arms across her chest and eyes me. "What's with the attitude, Zack?"

"You didn't ask me about moving here. I have no friends. And no driver's license. I had my learner's license in Alberta, Mom. Remember that little detail?"

She sighs. "I told you I was sorry about that. I am. But I had an opportunity, and I had to take it. Some day when you're older…"

"Almost a year older! Now I have to wait until I'm sixteen."

"Yes," she says. "You do. I know that might seem like a long time, but it will go by faster than you think. Especially if you keep busy. And you'll make friends in no time, Zack. You always do."

"Like that's going to happen while I'm stuck at home. With you." I stomp away into the garage. I find stakes and a hammer. I like the idea of pounding on something.

When I get back outside, Mom's gone. Her and her facts, she's big on those. Me, I'm not exactly against getting all the facts. But I definitely find other stuff more interesting.

I pound in the stakes, tie the string and start digging. As I dig, I consider what stuff I find interesting. I decide digging isn't among my interests. Girls, they're interesting. One of these days, I'll find one that thinks I'm interesting too. I'm pretty sure Charo likes me, but I don't think she's my type. She's nice enough, and she's average-looking. That would be okay if she didn't act so average too. She's always with her little group. She's got that pack mentality.

What's with that group-think stuff? I wish I knew. It seems like the groups here are tighter than any I've seen. I *have* always made friends, but this time it seems harder. Mom has moved us, what? Five times in the past twelve years? I used to think it would be easier if Dad was with us. Back around the second move, he said he wasn't coming. He was into a theatre group in Montreal and claimed he needed more time there. He told us he would catch up to us later. That was seven years ago, and he still hasn't caught up. I don't think he ever will.

I'm getting blisters from digging and decide gloves would be a good idea. I drop the shovel and go inside, where I find Mom isn't painting. She's sitting at the computer.

"So." I wave a hand. "Blisters here. How's it going for you?"

She gives me a look. "I'll finish the painting, Zack." She points at the computer. "But I wanted to check out this hobby I heard about. Geocaching. I think we're going to like it."

"We?" I ask.

"Yeah. It's pretty cool. You use a GPS device to hunt down treasure."

"Treasure?" I echo. "As in sunken pirate ships?"

"Not quite. Although who knows what we might find. See," she says, tapping the computer screen. "People all over the world are doing this. They put items in a box, called a geocache, and they hide it somewhere, cache it. Then they post the GPS coordinates online. Other people can use their GPS devices and find it."

"Yeah?" I say. "Well, I guess you'll have fun checking it out."

"I want you to help," she says.

"You think one of those boxes is hidden in our backyard?" I ask.

"No." She gives me a wry look. "Listen. I know this move has been hard on you. And I'm going to try to make sure we stay put, at least until you graduate. But you punching that kid—that's not like you. I'm disappointed, Zack."

"I can tell," I mutter.

"Yes, and you know I can't let it go. There have to be consequences. Your punishment stands. But I won't make you work the whole time you're grounded. And you can leave the house with me. What do you say we take a break and go try geocaching right now?"

If it gets me out of digging, I'm all for it. But I squint at her and go for a different sort of dig. "Before I say yes, maybe I should get a few more *details*."

Chapter Three

The geocaching website has hundreds of caches listed for Penticton. Mom picks one that's supposed to be easy to find. It's somewhere in a park she wants to check out.

She already has her handheld GPS device plugged in and charging. With this, we can receive signals from Global Positioning System satellites orbiting earth. Our next step is to enter the coordinates for the cache we want to find. The coordinates are numbers that pinpoint a position on the planet where lines of longitude and latitude intersect. All we have to do is find that intersection, and we should be within thirty feet of the cache.

Twenty minutes later, we're on our way. I'm navigating.

I check the display on the GPS device and see that we're picking up five satellite signals. Our current location isn't too far from where we want to go. But roads aren't built along the lines of longitude and latitude. As we drive, the road sometimes heads too far south, sometimes too far east. There isn't always a place to turn where we'd like, and sometimes I have to guess.

When we're on a road that follows the shore of Skaha Lake, Mom asks, "Are we close?"

"Closer than we were," I say. "But I think we should have taken the last turn."

She doesn't complain about me messing up. She just finds a place to turn around. Finally we're on a road that takes us uphill and ends in a parking area above the lake.

We get out of the car, and Mom is all smiles. "Look at that view."

"Cool," I say. It's a nice view, but I'm more interested in checking out the group of people on the far side of the parking lot. They look around my age. I'm hoping they're not kids from my school. I don't want to be seen hanging out with my mother.

"Okay, Zack," she says. Loudly. "Where do you think the cache is hidden?"

The kids turn to look. I withdraw into my hood, hoping to hide my face. "I don't know," I mutter. "You figure it out." I hand her the GPS.

I can feel her looking at me. Her voice is softer when she says, "I think we need to take that trail over there."

Luckily the trail is in the opposite direction from the group. Mom strides off, and I shuffle after her. We walk for about five minutes before she says, "It's got to be right around here."

"Yeah?" I don't see anything except dead grass, a few shrubs, pine trees and rocks.

"This is where our detecting skills come in," Mom says. "If you were hiding a small package, where would you put it?"

"I've never thought about it," I say. But I start searching. I can't help it. Something is hidden here, and I want to find it. I scan the ground for signs of tracks or disturbed earth. I don't see anything. I work my way up the hillside, checking shrubs and looking behind rocks. A few minutes later I spot a rotting stump. The top of the stump is covered with a chunk of log. I move the log aside and peer into the hole. "Got it."

I fish out a black garbage bag and open it. Mom comes over and watches as I pull out a small plastic box. It's labelled with a sticker that reads *Official Geocache*.

"What's inside?" Mom asks.

I'm curious too. I open the lid, and we start sifting through the contents. It's a big disappointment. There's a notebook with a pencil attached so we can record our names, and a bunch of kid stuff. I spot a Pokémon card, a little rubber ball and a plastic cow.

"Wow," I mutter.

"It's not about the treasure," Mom says. "It's the thrill of the hunt and where it takes you. I'll make a note in the logbook, and you go ahead and take your pick of the swag."

"The *swag*?" I ask.

"That's what geocachers call the items in the box. It's an acronym for Stuff We All Get. But the rule is if you take something out, you have to put something back."

"I don't have anything to put back," I tell her.

"I do." She grins and pulls a mini-calculator out of her pocket. "Don't look at me like that. The bank gave me this when I opened an account. Now go ahead and pick something."

"Jeez," I mutter. Sometimes I swear she thinks I'm still ten. "Let's see. Do I want the pen? The fish lure? Or how about this pineapple key chain?" I paw through the box and shake my head. "I don't want any of this." Then something on the bottom catches my eye. It's a CD in a plain sleeve. It looks like a blank. But when I turn it over, I find one word written in felt pen: *Famous*.

Huh. "I'll take this."

"There you go," Mom says. "Want to find another cache?"

"Um," I say. "I'm actually pretty hungry. Maybe we could go eat instead?"

Chapter Four

The first few days of being grounded were bad. After a couple more go by, I feel like I'm losing it. I play around with my guitar sometimes, watching the colors, but I can only do that for so long. I'm not that good at playing and probably never will be since I only play alone. It's tied in with my synesthesia and that makes it feel private.

When I was little, I assumed everyone saw colors with music. But when I got older and talked about it in school, the other kids laughed or called me a liar. Even Mom was confused when I went home and told her about it. She took me to the doctor and had me checked out. When we got the diagnosis, the doctor said I had a special gift. I should simply enjoy it. I decided he was right, but I also decided to keep it to myself.

When I've had enough guitar, I try other things. But watching TV or playing on the computer alone is boring. I've never been seriously into gaming, but I played sometimes with a couple of buds from the last town. I miss them. We're keeping in touch online, but it's not the same as having someone hang with you. I'm lonely and getting this restless feeling in my gut. I need to move or I'll explode. But I'm not allowed to blow off steam by going out to shoot hoops or play street hockey.

I'm almost wishing Mom hadn't eased back on the chore thing. That's how bad it's getting. She stopped by the school and picked up my homework. I was so desperate for something to do, I finished it right away. By Wednesday I'm lying on my bed, staring at the ceiling and plotting my escape.

But where can I go? And who can I see? There's nothing and no one. I pound on my pillow, then look around my room. It's a worse mess than normal. I haven't finished setting it up the way I'd like since we moved. I remember seeing some old shelves out in the garage, the sort you hang with brackets. Maybe I could put them up on my wall? They could hold my books and CDs. Most of my music is on my MP3 player, but sometimes I prefer the sound of CDs. I don't know why, but the colors are different.

Vinyl albums are different again. Live music is best.

I start sorting through the stuff on my floor, piling up clothes to make a work space. Under a pair of jeans I find the CD from the geocache. *Famous*. Huh. I'd forgotten about that. I decide it can't hurt to give it a listen. I stick it into my stereo and start stacking my other CDs.

Whoa! The sound filling my room is amazing. I freeze and watch indigo swirling like dark blue smoke. Incredible acoustic guitar music pours out of the speakers. It's like nothing I've ever heard. It must be a twelve-string. The player knows how to work it for all it's worth. Blue swirls and ripples of deep green flecked with brown move in.

The CDs I was holding fall to the floor, and I barely notice. And then this girl starts singing. Her voice is weak at first, a faded blue. But after a few bars her voice takes off and soars above the guitar. The blue I see now is a summer sky. I drop onto my bed to watch.

At first I'm so caught up in the sound I don't pay attention to the lyrics. But after a while I wonder what she's singing about. Lakes. Rivers. Traveling. The melody gives me the pink and gold of sunrises as she sings about taking off into the vast unknown.

When it ends, I need to hear it again. Now. But before I can move, another song starts. This one feels different. The guitar pauses between notes, building slowly. I see muted and misty shades of green, yellow and mauve—the colors of an old bruise. When her voice arrives, it's so uneven I can barely make out the words. I strain to catch them. The song is about loneliness. The vocals slip in and out of the guitar notes like they were supposed to be together but lost each other. It's as if the music is saying as much as or more than the words. I catch phrases about arriving alone, leaving alone. There's something about eternal solitude, about reaching for connection and always missing.

It's the saddest song I've ever heard.

There's an interval of static after the song ends, and I think that's the end of the CD. I get up to replay it, but then a third song starts. This one is jarring after the flow of the first two. The guitar strings aren't strummed and stroked. They're getting slammed. Purple and black form a backdrop for flashes of blood red. But again, the music fits the lyrics, because this one is about being used and lied to. It's about suspicion, about wanting to believe in someone. It's about wanting to trust and getting mocked instead. Feeling like a fool because everybody knew—except her.

It sounds like somebody messed her up. As the last guitar note fades to scabby brown, I hear a guy mutter, "Guess who."

I don't know why, but that ticks me off. How could he say that to her? Was it him that hurt her?

And who is she?

I listen to the songs again. By the second listen, I think maybe she's from Penticton because she mentions Skaha Lake.

By the third listen, I know I have to find her. This girl understands me better than I understand myself. I could never put into words what loneliness feels like, but she gets it. She knows what it feels like to be mocked. She knows what it feels like to want to go. Just go.

That last bit worries me. What if she stashed her CD in the geocache box and left? I imagine her with her guitar and a backpack at the side of the highway, thumb out for a ride. She'd be brave enough to do that. Anyone who creates music like hers, with lyrics that are so honest and so real, has got to have courage.

I want to find her. But how?

I take the CD out of the stereo and examine it. No clues there. Just that one word: *Famous*. I check the plastic sleeve it was in, and, again, there are no clues. I think back to when I found it in the geocache. Was there anything on the ground nearby? Not that I can recall.

What about the logbook in the cache box? Everyone is supposed to record their name there. All right. There's no guarantee that she wrote her name, but it's possible. Only how will I know which name is hers? Maybe it'll be obvious. Maybe she wrote that she left a CD. Or I'll see a name that *has* to be her.

I realize there's another clue. The handwriting on the CD would match the handwriting in the logbook, right? Not bad, Zack. Not bad at all. Maybe having a cop Mom who nags about *the details* has advantages.

Thinking about Mom makes me check the clock. It's too late for me to head out—she'll be home any time now. I'm going to have to wait until tomorrow. I *am* going, grounded or not. All I have to do is wait until Mom leaves for work and, bam, I'll be out the door. It only took about twenty minutes for us to drive to the cache site, including that wrong turn. I should be able to bike there in under an hour, easy.

Chapter Five

Mom doesn't leave for work until almost noon. It's a long morning. But it's good, because it means she won't come home for lunch.

She's barely out of the driveway when I'm out the back door. It's a cold, foggy day, not the sun-and-fun weather I'd expected in Penticton. I'd checked the city out online before we moved here.

Every site was all about the swimming, boating and beaches. There was no mention of the winter weather, which is cold, drizzly and dull.

I decide to look on the bright side. I can barely see the stop sign at the end of our street, but at least I'm out of the house and moving. I pedal as fast as the limited visibility allows, keeping my hands ready to grab the brakes. The pace and the feel of the CD in my pocket warm me, inside and out. I brought the CD along so I could match the handwriting, but having it with me feels like having a bit of *her* with me too.

Half an hour later I reach the road heading to the viewpoint. I see a trail veering off along the hillside and wonder if it's the same one the cache is on. It could be a shortcut, but I'm not sure. I decide not to risk it. I don't like being on the road, since Mom could cruise by—but what are the chances? And the fog might make it hard for me to see, but it's doing the same to everyone. I'm good.

And I am good. Another fifteen minutes of hard uphill pedaling, and I'm in the parking lot. There's no view of the lake today, but I'm not here for that. Minutes later I'm closing in on the cache. The straight trunks of the pine trees are spooky in the fog. Some are almost like the silhouettes of people. The only sound is my tires, crunching on the gravel path. When I get to the spot where I think the stump should be, I stop and look around. I can hear another sound now: steady dripping. The fog has condensed into water drops that fall from the pines like rain.

I get off my bike and stand there, straining to see the stump, uncertain about leaving the trail. It might be tough to find my way back. Then, like it was meant to be, a gust of wind parts the fog. And there's the stump. I bolt for it, and seconds later I've got the cache box in my hands. I pry open the lid, grab the logbook and start reading. The last entry in the book is Mom's, noting the date and our first names. I scan back from there.

The cache has been found quite a few times, mostly by families. They write about how they're having a great vacation and where they're from. Other entries are only a date and initials. I go all the way back to the first entry, written last April. This shows that the Wandering Woods family started the cache, and that's it. Nothing special catches my eye.

I comb through the logbook again, more slowly. This time I zero in on an entry from last October. It's the single letter *F*. It looks familiar. I pull out the CD, and sure enough, the *F* in *Famous* is identical. All right! But my moment of elation is short. So what if that's her initial?

I still don't know her name. And if she cached the CD last October, she could be long gone.

I toss the logbook back into the box and snap the lid shut. I put the box back in the stump and cover it with the chunk of wood. What a waste of time. I turn to go to the trail and don't see it. Great. I get to be lost now too? My stomach rumbles. I'm lost *and* hungry.

I know the trail is downhill from where I am. I look at the dead grass at my feet and can see some stalks that are trampled. It's all in the details. I follow the path of trampled grass, and my feet find the trail again.

I peer through the fog, back the way I came, then peer the other way. It makes sense that the trail would lead down to the road by the lake. I decide to take the trail down the hill. It's bound to be a faster way back.

It isn't. For starters, I can't ride. It's not only that the trail is narrow and steep. It's also that I can't see more than two feet ahead of me. If I don't keep my eyes glued to the ground, I risk losing the path altogether. When I do look up, my eyes strain to penetrate the silent wall of white. The fog coats my eyeballs. They sting, and the water and the cold make my nose run. I'm dripping like the trees. If this fog were music, what would it be? I've never heard music that looks like this.

When I come to a fork in the trail, I consider turning back. But that means dragging my bike uphill, and it feels like failure. I stand there thinking I should have brought the GPS. I decide that since the path to the left *seems* to go down, I should take it.

And then a sound comes out of the fog. It is so strange and piercing, all thought ceases. The hair on the back of my neck rises, and midnight blue ripples around me. I feel a million miles from anywhere and anyone, utterly alone. The sound repeats, and my brain comes back online. I realize the eerie, fluting call is made by a loon. I only know the sound from TV, but it's unmistakable. It's one of the musical bird calls that give me color. The loon calls again, and the midnight blue is a relief after the no-color of fog. I tilt my head, trying to pinpoint the loon's location. It must be close by. And it must be on the lake.

The calls stop as suddenly as they started, but they've guided me to go to the right. The trail is steeper and rougher than ever, and it's hard to hold on to my bouncing, bucking bike. But within minutes I've found the road. I'm so relieved I shout, "Yes!"

My voice sounds unnaturally loud, almost as startling as the loon. A glance at my watch shows I've been gone three hours. I'm going to have to hurry to make it home before Mom stops in on her dinner break.

I do make it. I throw my wet clothes in the wash and park my butt on the couch mere seconds before she comes through the door.

"What a day," she says.

"Bad?" I ask.

"One fender bender after another. It's this fog." She sighs and runs a hand through her hair. "I've only got time for a quick bite. Did you eat?"

"Not yet."

"Want to help me heat up some left-overs?" she asks.

"Sure." And that's it. We heat up meatloaf and vegetables, scarf it down, and then she's gone again. When I watch her leave, I notice my sopping sneakers by the back door. Mom didn't catch that evidence of my jailbreak. After I stick the shoes on a heat vent, I'm out of things to do.

TV? No. Video game? No. My girl's CD? Yeah.

I sit back with my eyes closed, watching her colors go by. Then I grab my guitar and strum along with her, watching our colors merge. They don't harmonize as well as I'd like. I'm not sure if it's because she's so much better, or because I'm trying too hard. But what if we could play together? In person. Wow. That would be epic.

I have to find her. But how? All I know is her name starts with the letter *F*. It would help if I knew what she looked like. I'll bet she's got red hair. Not carrot red, but that dark brown red. Auburn. Yeah, she's got auburn hair. I've seen that color in the music. And her hair is long and wavy. No, maybe short and spiky. Not short and spiky. It's long, for sure. But maybe it's black? It could be black. Whatever it is, it's thick and soft.

Her skin is perfect. Smooth and light brown. I'm not sure if it's light brown because she's tanned or because it just is. And her body? It's perfect too. She's tall, but not as tall as me. And she's slender, but not skinny. When I get close to her she smells like...

Jeez. No way does she smell like barf. I get off the couch and take my sneakers off the vent. That pretty much ruined my fantasy. It's time to get back to the facts.

Famous. Could that mean she *is* famous? I doubt it. I'd recognize most famous voices, at least if they're current. I spend the next few hours listening to female indie singers online. My search isn't methodical. I listen to almost a hundred singers, and none of them are her. A few have a similar sound, but they don't sing the CD songs. And none of them have names that start with *F*.

Chapter Six

After dinner on Friday, Mom says, "You've done your time, Zack. You're free to go."

It takes about three seconds for the words to sink in. When they do, I don't wait around to hear more. I grab my jacket and yell, "See ya," as I dive out the back door.

She follows me and yells, "Not so fast, mister. Where are you going?"

I have to think about that. Where am I going? "Maybe I'll take a bike ride." I detour toward the garage.

"I want you home by ten. Do you have your cell phone? Are your lights working?"

I don't answer until I'm outside with the bike, helmet on. I flick on the bike lights and wave my cell phone in the air. "See? It's all good."

I'm gone before she can ask me more questions.

I ride like a demon for the first twenty minutes. I don't have a destination in mind. I just go. When I finally slow down, I am at the far end of Main Street, close to the waterfront. Penticton sits between Skaha and the much larger Okanagan Lake. We live near Skaha. Okanagan Lake is where most of the stores are—and the people.

I'm looking for *her*. That seems crazy, even to me. But part of me believes that if I see her, I'll know. Some vibe will connect us. I get off my bike and push it along the sidewalk. It may be downtown on a Friday night, but the place is dead. The tourists aren't around in February, and that equals not much happening. Only a few restaurants are open.

Still, I need to look. I come across a music store and stop to stare in the window. There are some sweet guitars on display. I'll bet this is where she got her guitar. A flyer taped to the door catches my eye. It's advertising guitar lessons. Huh. Maybe I should take some. What if *she's* the instructor? I study the sheet of paper to see if there is a name, but there isn't. Still, it could be a lead worth checking. Then an awful thought occurs to me. What if she *is* the instructor and she's ten years older than me?

No way. That voice, it belongs to a girl around my age. I know it. This is like one of those hunches Mom talks about. She doesn't ignore them. She says you gotta go with your gut instincts. I'm going with my gut.

Another flyer advertises a gig featuring local musicians. It doesn't list all the performers, but the show is tomorrow night at the community center. Finally, a break. I am so going.

I hop on my bike and cruise down to the waterfront. I've still got a couple of hours before I have to be home. I pedal slowly, feeling more relaxed than I have in days. It's good to be outside. I notice a group of kids up the street and wonder if I know them. Probably not. But then one of the girls looks my way, and I recognize Charo.

She calls out, "Zack? Hey!"

I don't want to hear about my butt, so I crank my wheel to the right and pedal hard. I don't pay attention to where I'm going until I realize I've driven into a parking lot. When I stop to look around, I hear music.

It's not any music. It's the guitar melody of *her* traveling song. It's coming from the building in front of me. I'm almost at the door when I notice the sign: *Slick Sal's Neighborhood Pub.*

A pub? She's playing in a pub? I crane my neck to see inside, but the main door opens into a dark foyer. Should I go in? I could try. What's the big deal? I might be underage, but it's not like I'm going to try buying beer. I lean my bike against the wall, take a deep breath and go for it. I've made it to the doorway when the singing starts.

It's not her.

Some guy is singing *her* song.

Before I can wrap my head around that, a couple of people come up behind me.

"You mind letting us by, kid?" a guy asks.

"What?" I stammer.

He looks me over and shakes his head. "You haven't got a chance."

"Huh?" At first I think he means I haven't got a chance with *her*, but then I get it. "I was just listening to the music."

"Sure," he laughs. The woman beside him raises her eyebrows.

"Seriously," I say. "I know that song and I…Uh, would you mind doing me a favor?"

"I'm not booting for you," the guy says.

"No. That's not it. Could you ask that musician to come out here? Tell him I need to talk to him."

The guy squints at me and shakes his head again. "Look kid, I'm not a messenger boy. Take off." He brushes past me, the jerk.

But the woman pauses. "It looks like this is important. I'll ask one of the servers to pass along your message."

"Really? Thanks!"

"No promises. And if I were you," she adds, "I'd stay clear of the door. You don't want someone calling the cops."

I slink into the shadows alongside the building and wait.

Chapter Seven

I wait for over an hour, listening to the singer. He doesn't play any more of *her* songs, which is good—and not good. I don't think it's right for someone else to do her music, but I'd rather hear more of her stuff than his. The colors are different with him, deeper in tone, and duller too. The dullness is likely because the sound is muffled. But if he played her tunes, I'll bet the colors would be brighter, more vivid. I think about that to distract me from the fact that I'm getting cold and hungry. I'm ready to give up when the music stops.

Every muscle in my body tenses as I hear him say, "That's it for this set, folks. Time for me to take a break." There's a smattering of applause before the clatter of dishes and the murmur of voices take over.

Will he come out? I lurk around the corner from the door and watch. Some people do come out, including the couple I talked to earlier. They head straight for their car. I'm wondering if I should run after them to ask about my message when I hear something behind me. I turn and see a side door opening. Light spills into the parking lot, and a guy steps outside.

He looks the other way, then swings his head back and stares straight at me. He doesn't say anything.

"Hey," I croak. I clear my throat and step toward him. He's older than me, maybe around twenty or so, with long hair tied back in a ponytail. "Um," I manage. "Are you the performer?"

He lights a cigarette, takes a deep puff and slowly blows out the smoke. "Who wants to know?" he asks. Jeez. Major attitude.

"Me. I was wondering about one of the songs you sang."

He takes another drag. "What about it?"

"I've heard it before. And I'm looking for the girl who sings it."

His cigarette hand stops halfway to his mouth. "Say what?"

"The girl who sings that song about traveling and Skaha Lake," I explain. "I want to find her."

He laughs, but there's no joy in the sound. "You do, eh? Why's that?"

"Because." I shrug. "I do. I mean, I like her music. And I, uh, want to meet her. Do you know her?"

I have to wait through three more smoke drags before he mutters, "I used to."

Something about that sends a chill right into my bones. "Used to?" I choke. "She's not"—I can't bring myself to say *dead*—"gone, is she?"

He shrugs. "Not so far as I know. Last I heard, Jolene was working at a coffee joint over by the marina."

"Jolene?" I echo.

"Yeah," he says. "At least, I think that's who we're talking about."

"Does she sing there?" I ask.

"I doubt it. But then…" He pauses. "With her, could be."

"Is she there all the time?"

He drops his cigarette butt into a metal can by the door and says, "I don't know. I've gotta get going."

"Okay," I say. "Thanks, uh… whoever you are." I'm talking to a door.

Part of me is ticked off at the guy's attitude. But then the realization hits and sweeps all that away. I've found her!

Jolene.

It's the perfect name for her. So perfect, I should have *known* it. It must be her last name that starts with *F*.

The coffee shop by the marina. The marina isn't far from here. My phone shows I've still got half an hour. It's a no-brainer. I jump on my bike and go.

There are two coffee shops by the marina. One of them is a chain, the kind you see everywhere. The other, a café called Jumpin' Joe's Java, is closed. I wheel over to the window and glance inside. It looks like someone tried creating a tropical marine theme. Pictures of boats and brass anchors line the navy blue walls, and the counter is shaped like the prow of a ship. The tables are topped with grass umbrellas and fake parrots swinging on perches.

I'm almost certain Jolene wouldn't work in such a cheesy place, until I spot the music stand in the corner. A stool with a guitar propped beside it sits behind the stand, and suddenly the place doesn't look so cheesy. It has character, and this is where I'll find her tomorrow. The *J*s in the name are like a clue. It all adds up. In less than twenty-four hours, we'll meet.

I pull out my phone to check the time again. I've got seventeen minutes to make it home. There is no way I can risk getting grounded again. No way. I force my cold muscles to work hard, and luck is with me. The few traffic lights I hit are green, and I skid into the garage at exactly ten.

Mom squints when I come puffing into the kitchen. She points at the clock. It is one minute past the hour.

"I made it," I tell her. "I was in the garage on time."

She rolls her eyes, mutters something about cutting it close, but that's it. There's no Q and A. She just yawns and says she's going to bed because she's got an early shift tomorrow.

My luck is definitely changing. An early shift for her means I won't have to do the Q and A tomorrow morning either. Yeah, things are falling into place.

Chapter Eight

It takes a while for me to fall asleep.
I keep imagining meeting Jolene, and the
scene keeps changing. There's one with
me looking totally cool and walking up
to her, smiling. She smiles back, and we
start talking. It's as natural as breathing.
We walk out of the café, hand in hand.
And we don't care where our feet take
us, as long as we're together.

There's another scene, where she's not working at the café anymore. She's long gone. No one knows where she went. There's one where I trip and knock a hot coffee out of her hands, and it spills all over her guitar. Worst of all is the scene where I find her kissing another guy. I follow them to the marina, where they jump aboard his yacht and cruise off into the sunset.

I concentrate on the first scenario. I block out the others by playing her CD, turned down low, and closing my eyes. I finally doze off with the colors of her music drifting in my dreams.

In the morning I have a long shower, brush my teeth thoroughly and cut my chin when I decide to shave. I only have a bit of fuzz along my upper lip, so I don't know why I went for the chin. I stick a piece of toilet paper on the cut and have to wait almost half an hour before I can peel it off without bleeding again.

I wait another fifteen minutes to make sure. Finally I'm on my way.

When I get to Jumpin' Joe's Java, it looks packed. I lock my bike, take a deep breath and go inside. It turns out only the tables by the window are full. No one is playing the guitar. I steel myself to be cool and move toward the back without gawking. I sit with my back to the wall and casually look around.

I'll know her when I see her. I know I will. Maybe she'll know me too.

I feel someone's stare. When I turn my head, I meet the gaze of a woman with beefy arms planted on the counter. She lifts a weary hand and points to an overhead sign: *Place Orders Here.*

Right. I stand and saunter toward her but freeze when I notice a large gold *J* pinned to her apron.

No way. I gape at her, and she asks, "Is something wrong?"

"Uh..." I say.

She squints and says, "You want to order or not?"

"Jolene?" I croak.

"Excuse me?" she says.

I point at her apron. "Are you Jolene?"

"Look, kid, I've got things to do. If you're not going to order, then I'll get on with it."

"But..." My voice is barely more than a whisper. "Are you Jolene?"

She shakes her head. "I'm not Jolene. I've never heard of Jolene. Can I get you something or not?"

"You've never heard of Jolene?" I ask.

"Oh, Lord," she says. "I'm getting too old for this business." And she walks away.

I walk away too. Fast. I go out the door and get on my bike. Then I have to get off again to unlock it. I need to settle down. I pedal slowly over to the other coffee place. I decide my instincts were right the first time. Jolene wouldn't work in a cheesy place like Jumpin' Joe's.

Thinking that woman was my Jolene messed with my head. When I've got that freaky image blotted out, I square up my shoulders. Then I march through the door and head straight for the counter.

And there she is.

I know it's her. She's blond, she's pale and she's got violet blue eyes. She doesn't look the way I imagined, but she *is* gorgeous. When she says, "Can I help you?" I recognize her voice.

"Jolene." It's not a question. I simply state her name.

She frowns. "Do I know you?"

I summon a grin. "Not yet."

"Um," she says. And her bottom lip pouts. "Did you want coffee?"

"Jolene," I say, "I'm Zack. And I'm in love with…your music."

She blinks a few times, and then a small smile appears. "My music? You've heard it?"

I bob my head up and down. "Oh, yeah! It's fantastic."

Her smile widens. A dimple appears in her cheek. "Thanks. Where did you—?"

She's rudely cut off by the guy standing behind me. "Hey! I'm in a hurry. Can I get some service here?"

Everyone in the café turns to stare. Then a woman behind the counter rushes over. Her name tag reads *Manager*. "Is there a problem?"

"No," Jolene says. "I was just talking—"

The manager cuts in. "I've spoken to you before about visiting with your friends." She nods to the guy behind me. "I'm sorry. Can I take your order?"

It's my turn to cut in. "Excuse me. It's not Jolene's fault. I'm not her friend."

She raises her eyebrows. "And yet you know her name?"

"For pity's sake!" the guy behind me barks. "Can I get a tall dark and get out of here?"

"Of course," Jolene says sweetly. "Coming right up." She steps aside to pour the coffee, glances at me and asks, "And for you, sir?"

"Large mocha," I blurt. I look at the rude guy and deliberately add, "*Please*."

Jolene smiles, the manager shuffles away, the guy gets his coffee. As Jolene collects my money for the drink, she says, "I get a break in an hour. I'll be outside under the awning."

The next hour passes by in slow seconds, very slow seconds. I take my coffee outside and drink it. It leaves a bad taste in my mouth, so I go to a corner store and buy gum. Then I ride around, never going more than a block away. When the hour is finally up, I'm waiting under that awning when Jolene steps out the door.

Chapter Nine

Jolene walks straight toward me but stops before she gets too close. "Hey."

"Hey," I echo. Nothing else comes out of my mouth. My brain has gone blank.

"So," she says. "Zack, right?"

I manage a nod.

She takes a tiny step closer. "You wanted to tell me something about my music?"

"Yeah!" I wave my hands around as I struggle to speak. "It's freakin'... whoa. Amazing!"

She smiles. "Thanks. I'm wondering who...I mean, I don't think I've seen you before, have I?"

I keep nodding until I'm finally able to form a sentence. "I moved to town about a month ago."

Her smile fades as she asks, "So you live here?"

"Yeah," I say. For some reason I feel like apologizing. When she doesn't say anything else, I add, "Uh, is that a problem?"

She shrugs. "No. I was hoping you were from someplace else." She eyes me and says, "I did think you were a little young."

I ignore the part about me being young. She looks close to my age, maybe a bit older—not enough to matter. "Well, I *was* from someplace else but—"

She cuts me off. "*Where* exactly did you hear my music?"

"There was this guy who...but never mind him." I jam my hand into my jacket pocket and fish out the CD. I hold it up and say, "It was this. I heard you singing on this."

She snatches the CD out of my hand and stares at it as if she can't believe what she's seeing. Then her eyes flick up, and she nails me with a furious glare. "Where did you get this?"

"By the lake," I stammer. "On the hill. It was in this, uh, thing."

"A *thing*?" she asks.

"A geocache. It was part of the swag."

She shakes her head. "I have no clue what you're talking about."

"You mean you didn't put it there?" I ask.

"Why would I do that? It was the only copy. Someone took it. A long time ago, like, last fall."

"Really? That's terrible. Your only copy, huh?"

She nods. "Yeah." She tucks the CD into her purse and turns away.

"Wait!" I yelp.

She turns and raises her eyebrows. "My break's almost over. I have to go."

"But. Um. Maybe I could help you."

The eyebrows go higher. "You could help me?" she asks.

"Yeah. I love your music, you know. I could make you extra copies. I mean, I can't believe you're not already famous."

Her smile is back. "Yeah?" She hesitates for a moment, then pulls the CD out of her purse. "You'd make some copies for me? You can do that?"

"Absolutely. No problem. I'll burn them on my computer—as many as you want. You can send them out to radio stations. And maybe you could put it online, like other indie musicians. As soon as people hear this, they're going to want more."

I stop talking when she grabs my hand. "Wow, Zack. You think so?"

"Oh, yeah," I say. "I do."

She's still holding my hand, but her gaze is far away. "That's my dream. To do all that. But after the CD was taken, I gave up for a while."

"Why didn't you make another CD?" I ask.

She frowns. "I couldn't. I did some other stuff. Like, I went to auditions and things. But..." Her smile shines on me. "Maybe I can try again. With your help."

I feel warm all over. This is almost exactly the way I pictured it. I don't want to let go of her hand. I want us to start walking down the road to forever. But she pulls away, saying, "I have to go. Can we meet up later?"

"What? Yeah, for sure. That would be fantas—I mean, cool. Where should we meet?"

She shrugs. "You pick."

I scramble through the possibilities. I don't know what place would be good. I think of the pub, Slick Sal's, but that's stupid. "Should I come to your place?"

She shakes her head. "No way. I can't stand it there. How about yours?"

With my nosy cop mom hanging around? Right. The best I can come up with is a place within sight. "Would the burger joint over there," I say, pointing, "be okay?"

Her nose wrinkles. "Fine." She hands me the CD. "You'll bring the copies, right? What time?"

We agree on seven. She gets my cell number, and then she's gone. I stand there for a few minutes, letting it all sink in. I met her, at last. She's beautiful, like I knew she would be. And we're going out together…

I give my head a shake. We're meeting up again, yeah, but I don't think I came off like I wanted to. I was a starstruck idiot. I need to work on that. How?

I'm on my way home from the drugstore, a bag of blank CDs in hand, when it hits me. I should tell her how much I relate to her music. If I show her I get it, that I get *her*, then she'll get me. We'll have a real connection.

I spend the afternoon burning CDs. When Mom gets home, she gives me the Q and A. She's into it the second I tell her about my plans for tonight. I explain that I met Jolene in the coffee shop and we talked about music. Also that I found out Jolene is the singer on the geocache CD, but she didn't cache it. I don't tell any lies. I just leave out some details.

Then I ask, "How come you trusted me last night, and today you don't?"

"I trust *you*, Zack," she says. "It's others I have a problem with. What do you know about this girl?"

"I know she's smart and talented and a victim of crime. Who do you think stole her CD and put it in the geocache?"

Mom rolls her eyes. "Don't try to change the subject. Jolene works in a coffee shop. That's a good sign. Kids with jobs are usually responsible." She pauses and asks, "How long has she worked there? How old is she? Does she go to school?"

"Tell you what," I say. "I'll try to get all the *details* tonight if you stop bugging me now. Deal?"

She gives me her stink eye and mutters, "Deal." Then she sighs and adds, "I'm glad you've made a friend. I was invited out tonight, and I wasn't sure about leaving you alone."

"Mom. I'm fifteen, not five."

"I know, I know. But you've been stuck here alone too much." She glances at the clock. "I should get ready."

Chapter Ten

I'm on my way out the door when my cell phone rings. It's Jolene, and she whispers, "Zack?"

"Yeah?" Oh no. She's going to cancel.

"I, um…" Her voice catches on a sob.

I feel cold all over. "What's wrong? Jolene?"

"It's just—bad. I can't meet you. Oh god. I *really* need to get out of here."

Stories Mom has told me about domestic violence flash through my mind. "Are you hurt?" I ask.

"No. Not exactly. I just have to get out of here. Could you pick me up?" Her voice breaks again. "I need a ride."

She doesn't mean on a bike. "Jolene? Sorry, I don't know what to say." I do know what to say, but I'm stalling.

"Okay," she whispers. "Never mind. I'll try someone else. Bye."

I don't want her to hang up. "What about the CDs?"

"Oh. That. Maybe I'll be in touch…" I hear a muffled thump in the background. "I better go!" she squeaks.

"No! Wait!" I say. I have to do it. "I'll come and get you, okay? Tell me where you are. I'm on my way."

I can drive. Of course I can. The car is here. Mom won't know. What difference does a piece of paper make at a time like this?

"Are you sure?" Jolene asks.

"Absolutely," I say.

"You're a lifesaver. Okay, I'm going to start walking. Could you pick me up at the bottom of Heaven Hill Road? Past the high school."

"I know where it is," I say. "I'll be there in five minutes."

I don't allow myself to think about what I'm doing. I just do it. I get the spare car keys and run out to the car. I remember the CDs, run back inside, grab them and go.

Heaven Hill Road. How perfect is that for Jolene? I let myself think about that—and her. I drive at exactly the speed limit, and I'm there in five minutes. I park and look around.

I don't see her. What I do see in the rearview mirror is a cop car approaching. I slump down in the seat and turn my head away. I've only met a couple of Mom's new co-workers, but I'm not taking any chances. I sweat through the ten seconds it takes for the car to cruise past. Then I let out a breath I didn't know I was holding.

Two seconds later, a rap on the passenger window makes me jump, and I hit my head on the ceiling. I gape stupidly at Jolene. She's smiling as she pulls the door open.

"Surprised to see me?" she asks.

"Uh, yeah. I mean, no. Hi."

She hefts a backpack into the backseat and hops in beside me. She looks incredibly hot. Her hair flies in a fine, pale mist around her shoulders. She's lost the work apron, and without it there's no hiding her body. The tight jeans she's wearing, along with a form-hugging T-shirt and jacket…Wow.

She brings her scent in too, a heady mix of flowers and fruit. I breathe it in and ask, "Are you okay?"

"A lot better now that I'm here," she smiles.

I swallow hard and stare at her. She's here beside me. Incredible.

"So," she says. "Maybe we should get going."

I get a flash of my fantasy of Jolene and me heading into the unknown. This is quickly followed by a reality check. I have to get her wherever it is she's going, fast, and get the car back home. I don't tell her that. I nod and start the engine. "Uh. Where?"

"It's not far," she says. "Takes about half an hour."

"Half an hour?" I choke.

She turns those violet eyes on me, and they're huge. "That's okay, right?

I need to get somewhere safe. And it's the only place I could think of."

I consider taking her to my house. She'd be safe there. "My place would be—"

"No!" Jolene's voice has a frantic edge. "If you can't take me, then drop me off on the highway, okay? I'll hitch."

"What? No." I take a deep breath. I've come this far. I've already crossed the line. "Tell me the way. I'll take you."

Jolene smiles and settles back in her seat. "Okay, you want to get on the highway."

Five minutes later we're on the highway going north. I haven't done much highway driving, but it's actually easier than driving in town.

I want to ask Jolene what happened, but before I can, she asks, "Have you got the CDs?"

"On the backseat."

Jolene unbuckles her seat belt, turns around and reaches into the back. I stare at the curve of her body, and a front tire bounces as it hits gravel.

I gasp and swerve back to pavement. Jolene mutters, "Wow. Drive much?"

"I'm sorry," I say. I keep my eyes glued to the road.

She wriggles back into place and doesn't say anything.

"I'm sorry," I say again. When she still doesn't answer, I keep talking. "So, I burned twenty copies for you. I put the original in the bag. But I kept one at home for myself so actually there's only nineteen…"

"Why did you keep one?" she asks.

"Um. I thought it would be okay. Sorry. I can give you that one too, if you think…"

She waves a hand. "Never mind. Keep it. Not like you don't have it on your hard drive or whatever now anyway, right?"

"Right." A couple of uneasy moments pass, and I have to try again. "So, about your music, Jolene. I can totally relate."

"Yeah? What do you mean?"

"The song about traveling?" I risk glancing at her. "When I heard it, I wanted to hit the road. It got me thinking about how great it would be to see the world on my own terms. Be free. And the one about being alone? Wow."

"What about it?" she asks.

"It was like you could be me. I moved here and don't know anyone. It's tough."

"Yeah?" She shrugs. "I guess for some people. Not me. I can't wait to get out of this hick town. Like when I've gone on trips for auditions and stuff? I love that."

"So is your favorite song the traveling one?" I ask.

"I don't have favorites," she says.

"No? Huh. I guess you like them all for different reasons. Like the one about being made into a fool and mocked. The colors in it—I mean, I've experienced that too. It's harsh. I don't want to think about it. But you were able to put it into words."

I feel her stare, and then she mutters, "Yeah. But what about the singing?"

"What do you mean?" I ask.

"The singing. You know, the *voice*? I guess you don't know much about music. You haven't mentioned the quality of my sound."

"Oh," I say. Do I tell her how sound becomes color for me? I haven't risked that for a long time. Still, she's so honest in her music. I should be honest with her. "I see the sound in colors."

"What?"

"Colors. I'm a sound-color synesthete. The traveling song is indigo and green. And the rejection song is mostly black and red." I hold my breath and wait, hoping she'll understand.

She emits a tiny snort and says, "Yeah, right."

Chapter Eleven

I shouldn't have told Jolene about the colors. Not yet. I'm an idiot. I muster a feeble grin and shrug.

"So, you *don't* know much about music, do you?" she asks.

"I know what I like," I tell her. "And I know I like your stuff."

"Nice," she says. "But what about your ideas for promoting me?"

"Huh?"

She gives her hair an impatient flick. "You know. You talked about how I should send out my CDs. Do you know about that? Like, I just mail them to radio stations, or what?"

"I think so. I'm sure I've heard about that." I scramble for something else to say. "And I'm sure I could figure out how to put it online."

"Right. The indie thing. I knew a guy who—never mind. I'd rather have my career happen the old-school way. Like, I get discovered by a label, and they help me put together a band. And they promote it. All that. So all *I* have to do is perform."

"That makes sense," I say. "You're the artist. You shouldn't have to do all that other crap."

"Exactly," she says.

"Plus, that way you'll be free to write songs and play your guitar."

She doesn't answer.

I try again. "You've got all that depth and talent. You express feelings so clearly. It seems like such a gift. I mean, when you sang about being mocked and—"

"Tell me, Zack," she cuts in. "What is it about that song you relate to so much?"

I feel a flush crawl over my face. "It's stupid. It's not a heartbreak or anything. It was dumb. I was playing basketball, and some jerk pulled my shorts down. Then another jerk took a picture and posted it online. After that, everyone at school was mocking me."

I feel her stare. "That was you?" She laughs. It's the first time I've heard her laugh.

"You know about that?" I ask.

"Who doesn't? In a town this size, you can't fart without everybody knowing."

"Great," I mutter.

"It *was* funny," she says. "I don't get how that could bug you." She drums her fingers on the dash and shrugs. "So anyway. I just want to sing."

"Okay," I say.

She goes on. "I've done some big auditions, you know. I even did one in the States. I was born there, and I can't wait to go back." Her gaze fixes on a point down the road. "But it can't hurt to mail out CDs. It's something to do while I'm waiting for callbacks."

"Cool. If you like, I'll help you figure out where to send them." As I say this, I wish I could take the words back. What's up with that? I *do* want to help her. Don't I? But the way she's acting makes me wonder. The Jolene sitting beside me doesn't seem like the one who sings. I take a breath and say, "Can I ask you something?"

"What?"

"It's tricky to put into words. But, you're so *honest* in your music. I like that. Do you think maybe you say stuff in music that you can't talk about otherwise?"

She sighs and does some more finger drumming. Then she says, "You need to make a turn up here. See the sign for Summerland?"

I see it. I concentrate on doing everything right. I signal and make the turn. Jolene directs me to take another turn and another. We're working our way through the small town and up a hillside. A glance at the clock on the dash surprises me. More than half an hour has passed since we left Penticton.

"Are we almost there?" I ask.

"Almost," she says.

"Where exactly are we going?"

"To a friend's place. He's cool." She's leaning forward, like she can't wait.

"Um," I mutter. "About the CDs."

She picks up the bag and says, "Forget it, okay?"

"Huh?"

"I don't think you know much about the business."

She's got that right. And *I* know I'm blowing it with her, but I don't know why. Maybe I'm being too pushy?

Quietly I say, "I'm not trying to tell you what to do, Jolene. I bet it's tough to switch from composing to—"

"God!" She cuts me off. "Do I have to spell it out for you? I didn't write those songs, okay? I didn't play the guitar. I just sang. That's what I do. The *important* part."

Chapter Twelve

A sick feeling rolls through my gut. "You just sang?"

"Yup." Jolene checks her fingernails. "That's what I do."

"If you didn't write the songs, who did?" I ask.

"Does it matter?" she counters.

"Maybe," I say. "Aren't there laws? You can't just *take* someone else's music, can you? I mean, when I heard that guy doing your song at the pub—wait. Is this *his* music?"

"Probably. Was it a guy with a ponytail? And attitude?"

I nod.

"Frank. My ex. He's an idiot."

Frank. The initial *F* in the geocache log and on the CD. I shake my head and ask, "He wrote the music? And he played the guitar?"

"Yeah," she says. "So? Let me tell you something, Mr. Righteous. Before you go judging me, you should know the whole story. Frank wrote those songs for me. He was inspired by me. And he wanted *me* to sing them."

"But…"

"Frank doesn't care about fame. He has zero ambition. *Zero*. He's all about his *art*. Whatever that's supposed to mean. What difference does it make if I record his songs?"

"So," I say slowly, "what if one of his songs became a hit? Would he get paid?"

"How should I know?" she says.

"Would you give him credit for being the composer?" I ask.

"Why should I? If I go out there and bust my butt, why should I worry about him?" Her voice rises shrilly. "He doesn't want to be famous. So I'd cause him a problem if his name got known…" She pauses. "Right?"

I don't know what to say, but it doesn't matter. Jolene keeps talking. "I've got the recording now. It'll be my word against his. Pull over here. This is it."

I brake, hard, and pull off the road. It's a gravel road in the middle of nowhere. All I can see in the dark is one driveway curving through the trees. I turn and look at her. I take in the sulky set of her mouth. It's not a cute pout, not anymore. The flyaway blond hair? Peroxide. The violet blue eyes? I'm betting contact lenses.

"I shouldn't have burned those CDs," I say.

She clutches the bag, throws open the car door and jumps out. "Why not? I did the singing. The songs are *mine*. Who cares if I don't compose or play?"

I meet her angry stare straight on. "You do play...people."

She doesn't answer. She hauls her backpack out of the backseat, slams the door and stalks away.

I look at the dashboard. According to the clock, I'm a dead man. I'll never make it home in time. The smell of Jolene's perfume makes me feel sick, so I roll down my window. In the distance, I hear the sound of laughter. Her laughter. And then there's silence.

Lines from Jolene's song—*Frank's song*—play in my head: *You've made solitude feel eternal / What do I owe you for giving me that?*

It takes a while for me to find my way back through the maze of side roads. My phone starts ringing before I reach the highway. I don't stop to answer it.

The drive home seems to take longer than the drive out. I try not to think. But when I hit Penticton, I wonder if Mom contacted her pals at work to be on the lookout for me. Would she do that? She would.

I don't want to get caught by a cop. I don't want to go home and face Mom. But I'm going to have to do it sooner or later. It's better to get it over with. To avoid getting stopped, I think only about driving perfectly the rest of the way home.

Chapter Thirteen

When I get home, I'm braced for the rant of my life. I'm fully prepared for the possibility that Mom will have me charged with theft. She believes in consequences. Nothing prepares me for what happens when I walk inside.

She takes one look at me and crumples. Every part of her crumples— her eyes, her mouth, her entire body—

as she collapses into a chair. She buries her face in her hands and sobs.

I've never seen my mother cry like this. Never. And the way it makes me feel—I've never felt this either. Shocked. Scared. Ashamed. Sick. Sorry.

So sorry. I crouch on the floor in front of her and say it over and over.

Eventually she grabs my face with both hands and says, "Do you know how many kids I've seen broken in car wrecks? Do you?"

I don't. She never talks about that. And she doesn't now. She picks up her phone and goes into the kitchen to make a call so I don't hear what's said.

When she comes back, she's steadier. "Tell me what happened, Zack."

I tell her everything. When I'm done, she says she needs to think.

The next day I get the verdict. I have to enroll in swimming classes and can't stop until I'm a certified lifeguard. I have to complete a course in First Aid. And until the end of the school year, I'll do daily crossing-guard duty at an elementary school.

"Do you understand?" she asks.

The safety theme is obvious. I nod.

All day I resist listening to music. In the evening I start dreading going to school tomorrow. If they're going to mock me again, I do not want to go there.

Frank gets what it's like to be mocked.

Frank. And just like that, it's okay for me to listen to *his* songs again. This time, when I listen, I realize that it was never Jolene's voice I connected with. It was the lyrics and melodies. Her voice was only one small part. To be fair, she's a decent singer. I don't know. I'm no expert.

It's freaky how I'd built her up in my mind to be someone she isn't. I was practically in love with her. I don't get that. Maybe I'm a special sort of stupid.

What about Frank? He doesn't seem stupid. Jolene must have sucked him in too. That thought makes me feel better.

I don't feel much better, but it's enough to get me to school in the morning. I force myself to be totally casual as I walk into homeroom. A titter of laughter bursts from a group at the back, and I keep cool. I don't even look their way.

"Hey! Zack." Charo walks toward me. "I missed you." Here it comes. Some crack about my crack. But she says, "I thought I saw you downtown a few nights ago."

"Yeah?" I shrug.

"I guess it wasn't you. So how've you been?" she asks.

"Fine."

"Good. You know, I wanted to call you, but I couldn't find your number listed. I felt bad for you."

The group at the back laughs again, and Charo looks at them.

One of the girls calls, "Did you watch *American Idol* last night?"

Charo rolls her eyes. "Yeah." She starts to say something else, but the teacher walks in. She whispers, "Talk to you later, Zack." And then she takes her seat.

The morning goes like that. I hear people laugh, and I tune them out. Nobody openly mocks me, not once. The only thing related to my incident is a guy in PE who says, "Nice work punching out Perv Pete. He's done the same thing to a couple of girls—posted embarrassing pictures online, right? He had it coming."

Huh.

There's no lunch league game today, so I go to the cafeteria. I spot Charo across the room with her usual group. I decide to keep my distance. I notice a few guys from the team and head their way.

Before I can make it to them, Charo calls, "Zack. Over here."

I hate that her yelling has drawn attention to me. But if I try to ignore her, she'll probably yell louder. So I make my way toward her.

"Hey, Charo," I mutter.

"Hey, yourself." She frowns and asks, "Are you okay?"

Before I can answer, the girls in her group giggle and I tense up. Charo notices and says, "You need to relax. Let's sit down." She turns to her friends and tells them she'll catch up with them later.

When we're seated, she sighs. "I've heard enough about that *Idol* thing.

I don't know how they can still be chirping about it."

"*Idol* thing?" I ask.

"Come on," she says. "That's all everyone's talked about all morning. You must have heard people laughing?"

I shrug.

She squints at me like she's checking to see if I'm serious. I must pass her test because she says, "It's this girl who used to go to school here. She dropped out last year, so you wouldn't know her. She was on *American Idol* last night, doing an audition."

Chapter Fourteen

A girl from Penticton doing an audition in the States. I stare at Charo and ask, "How did she do?"

Charo rolls her eyes. "Terrible. She was wearing a black leather microskirt and a bra top. Like that would impress them. When she sang, it wasn't *that* bad. I mean, she did okay. Even the judges said so. But when they told her she needs to work on her voice, wow. She went off! They had to beep out almost everything she said. She didn't stop swearing until they called security."

"Huh."

Charo shakes her head. "In a way, it's sad. I was friends with her until last year. Then she got, I don't know, twisted or something. All she cared about was being famous."

"That's too bad," I say. "But it sounds like she did it to herself."

Charo nods. "I guess. But I don't get it. Why would someone do that?"

"I don't know." I shrug. We're quiet for a minute. I watch Charo chew her lip, trying to figure it out. Then I realize when she's not chewing on her lip, it's quivering. "Hey," I say. "Are you okay?"

"Yeah. Sorry. I was just thinking about how she must feel right now.

I heard she left town in case this happened. I guess they tape auditions, and you don't know if they'll show yours until it's on TV. She must have been hoping they wouldn't show her."

"I'll bet," I mutter.

She sighs. "By now she knows everyone saw it. Or if they didn't catch it on TV, they'll be watching it online."

I cover up my guilt. I definitely plan to check out Jolene's performance. "I'll bet she feels pretty bad," I say. "Unless…"

"Unless what?" Charo asks.

"What if she likes it? Doesn't this make her famous?"

Charo's mouth forms a small circle. "I never thought of it that way. I mean, this is more what you'd call being *in*famous. But with her, you never know."

We talk more, and it dawns on me that Charo isn't the average lemming

I assumed she was. She's interesting. It turns out she used to play keyboards in a girl garage band with Jolene.

Huh.

I tell her, "I play around with a guitar sometimes."

"Really?" she grins. "We should get together sometime and jam. Just for fun."

I don't make any promises, but when I head home later I think, maybe. I also think about how people have forgotten my stupid drama. Was it eclipsed by Jolene? Maybe fame is nothing more than talk. When we flock around the latest thing, do *we* create the fame—then take it away when we move on?

I don't know. But I do know I have to watch the video of Jolene. I didn't like it when everyone ogled my picture, but I'm not so above it. I have a cruel wish to see Jolene make a fool of herself.

The video clip is everything Charo described. It's not pretty. The colors I get with her song are bad. I see beige with a few dull streaks of pink as she wobbles through a pop tune. And Jolene's reaction to the judges is crazy.

But if fame is all Jolene wanted, she got it. The video has recorded thousands of hits. There are lots of comments too, most of them nasty. I'm about to close the site when a name catches my eye. Frank. He wrote, *I tried to tell you the same thing.* I bet that means he too tried to tell her that she wasn't ready.

Watching Jolene fail doesn't make me feel any better. If anything, I feel sorry for her. She's one seriously screwed-up girl.

And I was one screwed-up guy. Jolene played me for a fool, but I set myself up for it. Why? Was it being bored and lonely? The music?

Frank's music.

I have to tell Frank about burning those CDs before they burn a hole in my conscience. I call Slick Sal's, and they tell me he doesn't play there anymore. And no, they can't tell me where I can find him.

So now what? I'm not ready for another round of playing detective. I try to pump myself up for the search by remembering I found Jolene without so much as a name. How hard can it be to find Frank?

This time, my motivation isn't quite the same. Lurking outside pubs in the dark, hoping to find an angry guy, doesn't sound like fun. There has to be a better way.

It turns out I don't have to find Frank. A couple of weeks later, he finds me.

Chapter Fifteen

I'm sitting on the hillside at the geocache site, looking at Skaha Lake. I'm hoping to hear a loon again. I've got my guitar and I'm idly plucking strings, watching the pops of color. Suddenly Frank is on the trail, staring at me.

"Uh," I choke. "It's you."

"Yeah," he says. "Did you find her?"

I nod.

He lights a cigarette, then squints at me through the smoke. "And?"

"And nothing. At least, nothing much."

His smile is fleeting. "I could have told you there wouldn't be much."

"I know," I tell him.

His eyebrows go up. "How do you know what I know?"

He doesn't have the same attitude as when I met him. He seems curious. "I know you wrote the songs. And I know why."

"She told you about that?" He sounds surprised.

"She didn't exactly volunteer the information," I mutter.

"Interesting." He takes a drag on his cigarette, then says, "Ever since you asked about her, I've wondered where you heard her. Looks like I guessed right."

I nod.

He grins. "So you're a geocacher?"

"I tried it."

"Cool," Frank says. "And cool for me to know where the CD went. You know how you put stuff into caches and then wonder who has it now?"

"So you put that CD in there, right?" I ask.

He nods.

"Yeah, well, about that." I take a breath. "I have to tell you...Actually, first, I'd like to know...Why did you leave the CD here?"

Frank shrugs. "I didn't want it anymore. Too many bad memories. But it didn't feel right to toss it. Then I got this idea."

"What idea?" I ask.

"It was an experiment. It was like caching my feelings about that music. I thought I might get a song out of caching it."

"I think I get what you're saying. Did it work?" I ask. "Did you get a new song?"

Frank frowns. "Not yet. Inspiration happens in its own time. But I was thinking I should have made that CD a hitchhiker."

"A hitchhiker?" I ask.

"You can attach an extra logbook to an item, asking that it be carried to another cache. The people who take it along write a note in the log about where they found it. They can also post its new location on the geocache website. Then everyone can track the item's movements. Hitchhiking would've suited that CD."

I stare at him as I work out what he's implying. Then I laugh. "I get that."

My smile fades as I remember what I have to tell him. "About that CD. You don't mind if other people hear it?"

K.L. Denman

"Isn't that what music's for?" he asks.

"But what if Jolene takes credit for it? Wouldn't you mind that?"

He shakes his head. "Man, I don't care. She can sing those songs if she wants."

"But...I gave her the CD. And I made copies for her to send out to radio stations. I don't think she plans to tell anyone it's your music."

Frank goes quiet.

I wait.

Finally he sighs. "Whatever, man. I doubt Jolene will get around to doing that. But if by some miracle she gets to do a pro recording...I'll worry about it then. The only song I still do is 'Travel Time.' She can have the other two."

"'Travel Time,'" I echo. "I like that one."

"Yeah? It's all right, isn't it?" Frank gazes down the trail. "Speaking of, I should get going. Nice talking to you, uh…"

"Zack," I tell him. "Good talking to you too. Maybe I'll see you around? Out geocaching or something."

"I'm off and on with the caching," he says. "I mainly like the symbolism, you know? I like the idea of being able to pinpoint a position. Can't always do that with a lot of stuff we get."

I watch him walk away. Then I look at the sky and think about satellites. They're circling the globe, sending out signals, helping people everywhere find their position. I've seen them at night, twinkly points of light that could pass for stars. Only their behavior betrays that they're not real stars.

Jolene's like a satellite.

And me? I think I've pinpointed my position on a few things. I strum my guitar and watch the colors float over the lake. For now, this is exactly where I want to be.

Acknowledgments

My gratitude to authors Shelley Hrdlitschka and Diane Tullson, whose coordinates always read *friend* and *true*. Many thanks also to Melanie Jeffs, Orca editor, for her fine attention to the details.

K.L. Denman is the author of numerous popular and award-winning books for youth. Her previous works include *Rebel's Tag, Mirror Image, The Shade* and *Perfect Revenge* in the Orca Currents series, and the Governor General's Award nominee *Me, Myself and Ike*. She lives in Powell River, British Columbia.

orca *currents*

9781554694341 $9.95 pb
9781554698882 $16.95 lib

In most ways, Poe is like the other kids in his school. He thinks about girls and tries to avoid too much contact with teachers. He has a loving father who helps him with his homework. But Poe has a secret, and almost every day some small act threatens to expose him. He doesn't have a phone number to give to friends. He doesn't have an address. Poe and his father are living in a tent on city land. When the city clears the land to build housing, Poe worries that they might not be able to find another site near his school. Will Poe have to expose his secret to get help for himself and his father?

orca *currents*

9781554699032 $9.95 pb
9781554699049 $16.95 lib

At a Battle of the Bands event,
Ace and his best friend Denny notice that girls
like musicians, no matter how dorky the dudes
might be. So they start a band, and Ace discovers
that he loves playing music more than anything
he's done in his life. Fueled by Denny's tweets
and a sound guaranteed to make cats barf, the
band takes flight until a contest draws them into
conflict. Their drummer, Pig, cares more about
hygiene than music, and Denny's drive to impress
the girls leads them all astray.

orca currents

For more information on all the books
in the Orca Currents series, please visit
www.orcabook.com